This Little Tiger book belongs to:

_____

_____

_____

For Holly, with love ~ K W

To my beloved Grand-Maman.
Click, Clack, Croc' Geneviève! ~ J D

LITTLE TIGER PRESS LTD,
an imprint of the Little Tiger Group
1 Coda Studios, 189 Munster Road, London SW6 6AW
www.littletiger.co.uk

First published in Great Britain 2009
This edition published 2016

A CIP catalogue record for this book is available from
the British Library

All rights reserved · ISBN 978-1-84869-505-4

Printed in China · LTP/1800/3412/0820

10 9 8 7 6 5 4 3

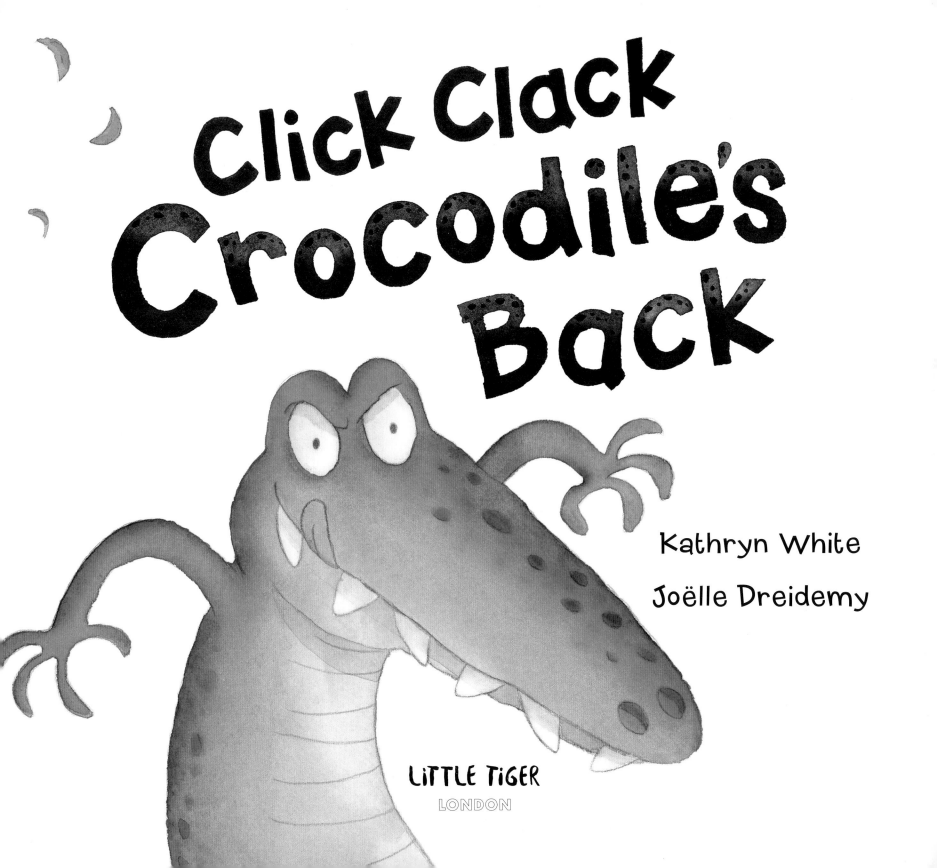

Click Clack Crocodile's Back

Kathryn White

Joëlle Dreidemy

LiTTLE TiGER
LONDON

Tremble with fear, Crocodile's near.
He's sneaking by, with a glint in his eye,
Slyly disguised as the trunk of a tree,
Ready to **snatch** you and **eat** you for tea!

Slip,
slap,
  it's Crocodile's trap.
He's **squelching**
and **sliding**
in mud, where he's hiding . . .

Waiting to **snaffle** you
up in his claws
And **gobble** you down
with his terrible jaws!

WATCH OUT,
Crocodile's about!
Flamingos are **Preening**
then one of them spies,

Down in the rushes,
two **mean,**
greedy eyes . . .

"LOOK OUT, IT'S CROCODILE!"

everyone cries.

"He keeps **creeping** up on me," Elephant groans. "That **big, sneaky** Crocodile," everyone moans.

But Monkey is cool,
Monkey is clever –
He has a plan they can
all do together.

So brave little Monkey swings down to the river.

"A gift for Crocodile," he says with a shiver.

"A **gift**?" says Crocodile,
very unsure.
"Why . . . I've never been
given a **gift** before."

Monkey holds out his **trembling** hand.
"This present will make you look
wonderfully grand.
It's a jacket I made from banana peel."

Crocodile grins
and says,
"Simply ideal!"

"We've made you a hat!" the flamingos flock in,
Making a **mess** and a terrible **din**.

And Crocodile roars,
"Oh, won't I look great?
I'll be **dashing** and **sporty**
and so **up-to-date!**"

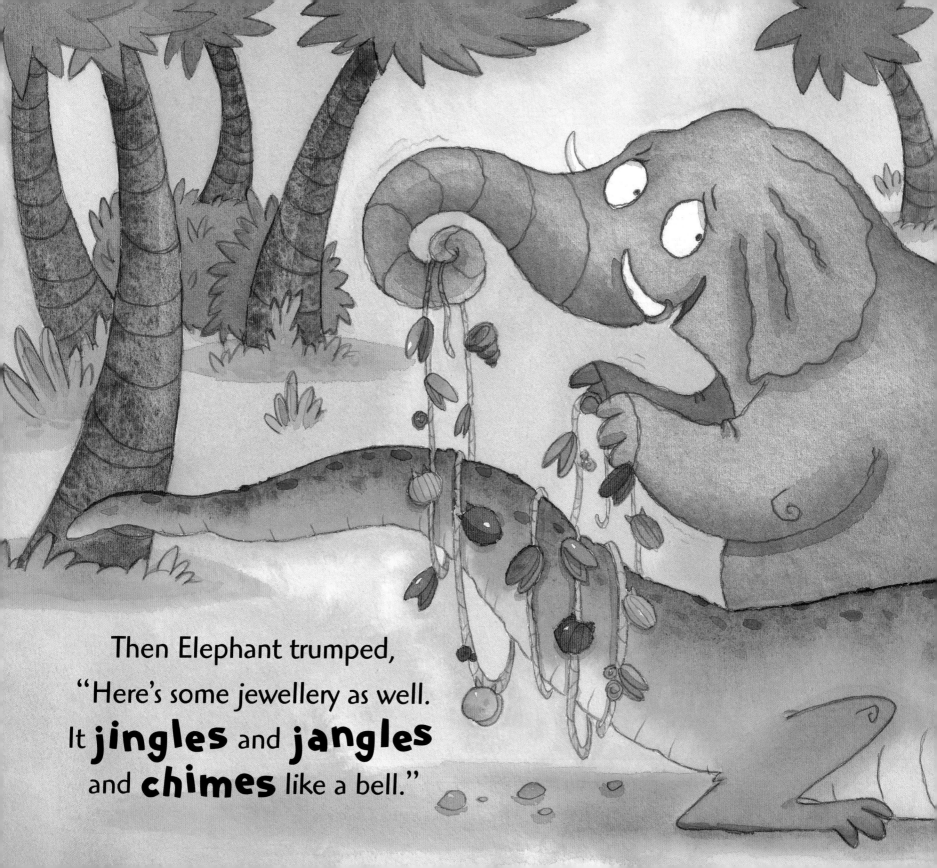

Then Elephant trumped,
"Here's some jewellery as well.
It **jingles** and **jangles**
and **chimes** like a bell."

"OH WOW,"
says Crocodile.
"How splendid I'll be,
When I **sneak** and I **creep**
and I **hunt** for my tea."

"And won't you
look **fabulous**,"
everyone cheers,

"When you wear these
new coconut charms
on your ears?"

"Awesome!" says Crocodile,
giving a

grrrowl,

"I'll wear them each time
I go out on the **prowl**."

So Crocodile grinned
and his **greedy** eyes shone,
As he shot off to try
all his new presents on.

Shhhhh!

Listen – what's making that sound?

It's **jingling** and **jangling** and **prowling** around.

We're **shaking** and **quaking**,
we're so **terrified!**

It's a wild, crazy animal.
RUN FOR IT! HIDE!

Click, clack, Crocodile's back!
In his necklace and jacket, and earrings and hat.
He looks just **fantastic,**
but he's **cross** as can be.
For everyone's hiding – and he can't catch his tea!